THE MAGICIAN'S WIFE

THE MAGICIAN'S WIFE

by Jerome Charyn
Illustrated by Françoise Boucq

Published by Catalan Communications
43 East 19th Street
New York, NY 10003

ISBN 0-87416-045-6
Dep. L.B. 32.064/87

First Printing September 1987
Printed in Catalonia (Spain) by JTV - Alvagraf

THE MAGICIAN'S WIFE

JEROME CHARYN FRANÇOIS BOUCQ

catalan communications
new york

A Note to the American Reader

I was reared by Donald Duck.

Having had a father who could barely growl any English and a mother who was always busy scrubbing walls, I received my instruction from comic books. It was Walt Disney who taught me how to read. I graduated to Captain Marvel, detesting Superman, who couldn't even shout ‹Shazam», and was inferior to Marvel in every way. I seized my diploma from Classic Comics, illustrated versions of Dickens and Dumas, but I had nowhere else to go.

I made the situation worse by becoming a scribbler myself, while I longed for the authenticity of the Three Musketeers jumping from panel to panel and clutching swords I could see. There were no comic books for adults in my neighborhood, except bits and pieces of pornography, and I wasn't interested in genitals surrounded by colored ink.

I rediscovered comic books in France, where the art is much too serious to be wasted on kids. Paris is a country of comic books, or *bandes dessinées*, as they are called. Comic books don't occupy some literary lower depth, as they do in the United States. The French are as involved with the bande dessinée as they are with Proust and Colette, Céline or Sartre. Each January they hold a festival of comic books at the medieval town of Angoulême, which is attended by 200,000 rabid admirers and fans, including the French minister of culture. A special jury awards the Prix Alfred to the best comic book of the year. The hurly-burly attached to this award is a bit like the hullabaloo of Oscar night in Hollywood. In 1986 the Alfred was given to *La Femme du magicien* (The Magician's Wife), the work of a young French illustrator from Lille, François Boucq, and a thin, slouching American novelist, Jerome Charyn.

La Femme du magicien soon began to sell all over the world. But even the French were mystified. How did this peculiar «marriage» take place? It wasn't peculiar at all. Visiting Paris five or six years ago, I fell in love with the bande dessinée and became a follower of «A Suivre», one of the French monthlies devoted to comic strips. I bullied its editor, Jean-Paul Mougin, into letting me join that singular club of comic-book artists and writers. I had the bones of a novel (about a lady werewolf) that I'd abandoned years ago. I turned it into a scenario and handed it to Mougin. He found Boucq. We wrangled, gestured, talked in pidgin English and French.

He started scratching away at the characters. I flew back to Paris once or twice. And *La Femme du magicien* began to find a shape.

Boucq is a kendo expert. I'm a former Bronx thug. But we managed not to injure one another. The book appeared and received a firestorm of praise (about four hundred reviews). It was adored... and attacked, of course. But I didn't care. I'd cashed in on my education. I'd returned to the land of Donald Duck.

There are signs that this new French Revolution is beginning to reach the United States. The French took an American art form, the comic strip, caressed it, and made it their own. Their very best works—by Bilal, Boucq, Tardi, Masse, Liberatore (an Italian living in Paris), Loustal —is as complicated and perverse as any other kind of fiction. And the idea of the graphic novel, which Americans have resisted for so long, now seems a little less irregular or remote.

Whatever the fate of *The Magician's Wife*, the bande dessinée is a form *and* a phenomenon that will have to be reckoned with.

Jerome Charyn
March 1987

CHAPTER 1

SARATOGA SPRINGS 1956

HEY FRANK, WHAT THE HELL'S THE MATTER?

NOTHIN'... MUST BE THE HEAT.

I'M THIRSTY. I NEED A GODDAMN GLASS OF WATER.

HEY, ANYBODY INSIDE?

HELLO, PRINCESS!

YOU HAVE A LITTLE WATER FOR A POOR OL' COWBOY WHO'S BEEN OUT IN THE SUN?

DON'T GO AWAY.

I'LL BRING YOU A BIG GLASS.

EDMUND, MY DEAR. I HAVE SOMETHING TO SAY...

YOU'LL NEVER MAKE A LIVING WITH YOUR MAGIC TRICKS.

IF I WERE YOUR FATHER, I WOULD FORCE YOU TO GO BACK TO SCHOOL.

WHAT KIND OF A FUTURE IS THERE IN A MAGICIAN'S HAT?

YOU SHOULD HELP YOUR FATHER FIX THE ROOF INSTEAD OF BOTHERING MRS. WEDNESDAY WITH ALL YOUR IMBICILITIES.

SHE CAN'T BE YOUR AUDIENCE, EDMUND. NO, NO, NO.

SHE HAS A HOUSE TO CLEAN...

OUT OF THERE, BOTH OF YOU, BEFORE I CHASE YOU OUT.

I KNOW YOU... YOU'RE DOLORES.

HE'S NOT DOLORES. DOES HE LOOK LIKE DOLORES?

DOLORES! DOLORES!

I'M SORRY. DIDN'T MEAN TO INSULT YOU, SIR.

HELLO, RITA!

WHY DO YOU ALWAYS HAVE TO FRIGHTEN ME, EDMUND?

BECAUSE I'M IN LOVE WITH YOU, MISSY...

13

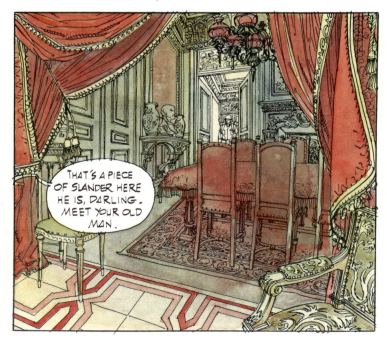

16

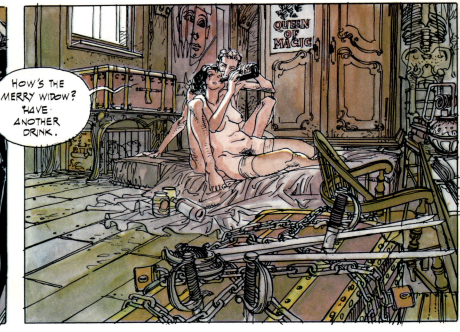

HOW'S THE MERRY WIDOW? HAVE ANOTHER DRINK.

EDMUND, THAT'S ENOUGH.

DON'T YOU WORRY, LOVE.

I'LL TAKE YOU AND YOUR DARLING DAUGHTER AWAY FROM HERE. IT'S A MAUSOLEUM. MY FATHER WILL DIE UP ON HIS ROOF AND NO ONE WILL EVER MISS HIM. MOTHER HASN'T SAID A WORD TO HIM IN THREE YEARS.

EDMUND, THEY'VE BEEN NICE TO ME. I CAN'T LEAVE JUST LIKE THAT.

THEY PUT YOU IN THE KITCHEN AND YOU CALL THAT NICE?

YOU DON'T KNOW WHAT NICE IS.

EDMUND, PLEASE... I HAVE RITA TO SUPPORT.

HOW WILL WE LIVE? YOU'VE NEVER WORKED. YOU'RE STILL HALF A CHILD.

HALF A CHILD? I'LL SHOW YOU WHAT HALF A CHILD CAN DO.

GET AWAY FROM ME!

MOSCOW 1960

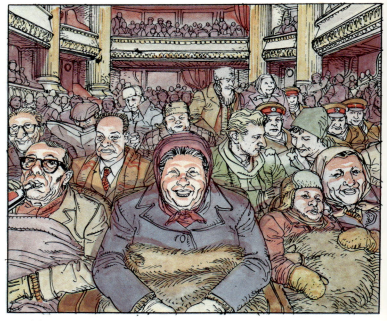

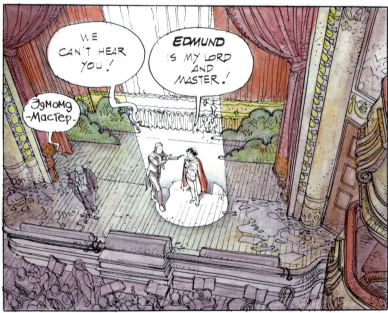

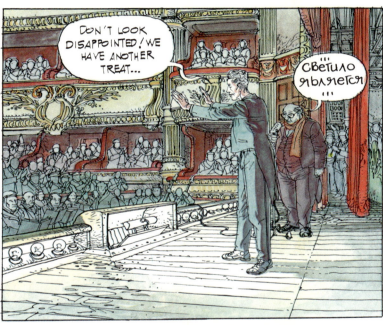

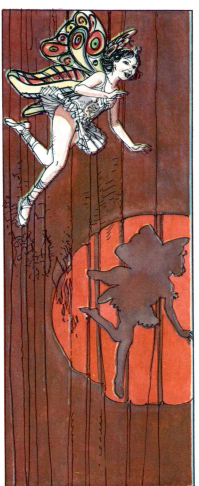

PARIS 1962

MONTH AFTER MONTH, RITA BECOMES MORE AND MORE BEAUTIFUL.

AFTER, YOU'RE FINISHED, WE'LL WALK ON THE QUAY. YOU'LL LOVE IT THERE!

I'M NOT SURE..MAMA LOOKS TIRED.

OH, YES, POOR MAMA. SHE OUGHT TO TRY THE SNAILS.

BUT WE HAVE TO FATTEN YOU UP.

I CAN'T... I'M NOT HUNGRY.

THE SNAILS WILL GIVE YOU A BIT OF COLOR. I'M GOING TO LET YOU RIDE RUPERT.

EDMUND, MAMA'S TOO OLD FOR PONIES.

YOU'RE RIGHT, DUCK. YOUR MOTHER IS MUCH TOO OLD. MAYBE SHE COULD BE YOUR DRESSER...

... SHE WOULD MAKE A PERFECT DRESSER... AND A MAID.

CAIRO

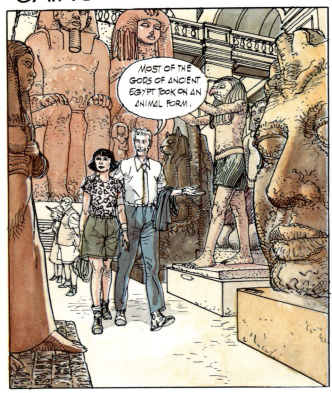

MOST OF THE GODS OF ANCIENT EGYPT TOOK ON AN ANIMAL FORM.

...HORUS WITH A FALCON'S HEAD. HIS EYES WERE SUPPOSED TO BE THE SUN AND THE MOON...

BUT THE MOST DISTURBING ONE WAS ANUBIS, THE WOLF GOD. HE GUARDED ALL THE TOMBS.

LONDON 1963

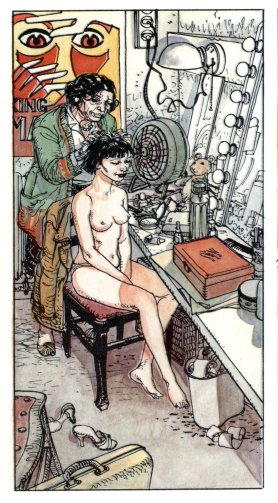

MOTHER, IT'S SILLY TO SIT IN THE DRESSING ROOM ALL THE TIME. EDMUND CAN WORK YOU INTO THE ACT AGAIN.

NO, RITA. I'D RATHER STAY HERE.

MY TWO LITTLE COWS ARE CONSPIRING AGAIN. DON'T FORGET, NOTHING CAN ESCAPE A MAGICIAN.

EDMUND DOESN'T WANT TO HAVE ME AROUND.

You're mine, Miss Wednesday. You can't take your eyes off this glove. You're getting sleepy.

You can hear nothing, nothing but my voice. And you can't resist.

You're soft and sweet, like a baby lamb that's just come out of its mama's belly.

And now, good people, our little lamb is going to skip in front of you and perform lots of delicious leaps.

RITA...

STOP, RITA! I LOVE YOU...

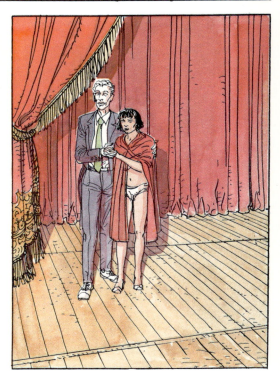

CHAPTER 2

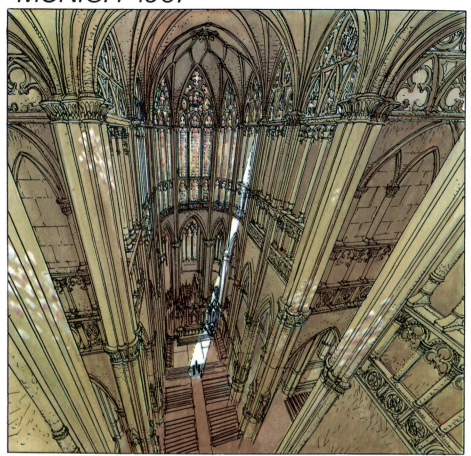

STAY OUT OF THIS, DARLING. IT'S BETWEEN YOUR MOTHER AND ME.

IF YOU THROW HER OUT, YOU'LL LOSE YOUR LITTLE MISS WEDNESDAY. I WON'T PERFORM.

YOU'LL PERFORM. I COULD HYPNOTIZE YOU, TURN YOU INTO A PONY.

THEN THE PONY WILL LIE DOWN AND STOP PERFORMING... MAMA STAYS.

THE FEVER OF PERFORMING SEEMS TO HOLD TOGETHER THIS STRANGE MENAGERIE.

A CAPTIVE TO HER OWN SUCCESS, RITA HAS BECOME A STAGE "ANIMAL" WHO THRIVES ON PUBLIC ATTENTION AND APPLAUSE.

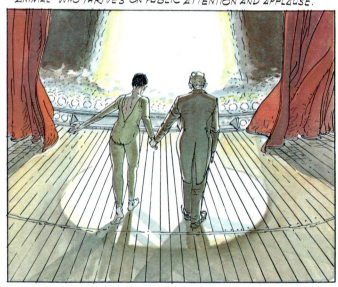

EXCUSE ME! PLEASE LET ME THROUGH. MADAME RITA, MADAME RITA!

I'VE COME FROM THE HOTEL. MADAME RITA, YOU MOTHER...I'M SO SORRY.

35

THERE WAS NOTHING I COULD DO, MADAME...I FOUND HER DEAD.

MADAME'S MOTHER DIED WITHOUT SUFFERING. IF SHE HAD COUGHED OR STARTED TO TO CHOKE, DOLORES WOULD HAVE HEARD.

WHO'S DOLORES?

SHE'S THE MAID ON THIS FLOOR. IT WAS DOLORES WHO DISCOVERED THE BODY. NOTHING EVER HAPPENS WITHOUT DOLORES.

YOU KILLED HER!

IT WAS YOU! YOU TOOK HER LIFE AWAY, BIT BY BIT.

REALLY? AND WHO WAS MY ACCOMPLICE, EH?

YOU SON OF A BITCH.!!

RITA, STOP! YOU'RE BEHAVING LIKE A WILD DOG. EVERYTHING I DID WAS FOR YOU... FOR YOU.

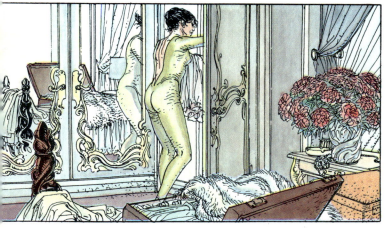

COME, MY BEAUTY, COME WITH US. WE'LL WARM UP YOUR TIGHT LITTLE HEART.

...LIFE IS MUCH TOO SHORT TO WEAR SUCH A LONG FACE.

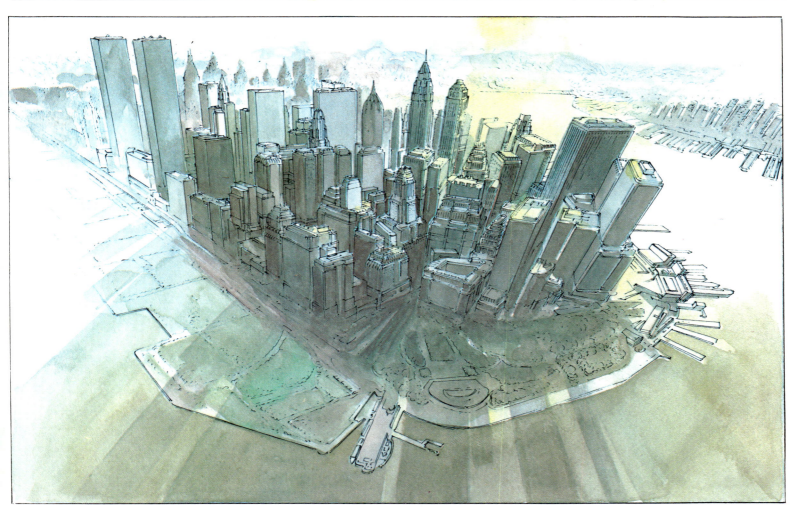

41

RITA LIVED IN A SMALL FURNISHED ROOM NEAR CENTRAL PARK. SHE WENT FROM ONE ROUTINE TO THE NEXT, DAY AFTER DAY.

RITA HAD BECOME A GIRL WHO NEVER SMILES.

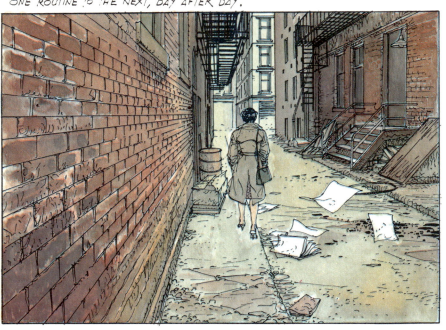

42

SHE WASTED ENDLESS HOURS LOOKING AT THE WALL OUTSIDE HER WINDOW. IMAGES OUT OF HER LIFE WOULD APPEAR ON THE WALL, AS IF IT WERE A SCREEN THAT COULD CONTAIN THE CORNERS OF HER MEMORY IN ALL THE CRACKED BRICKS.

EDMUND CAN'T FIND ME. I'LL NEVER GO BACK TO HIM. NEVER!

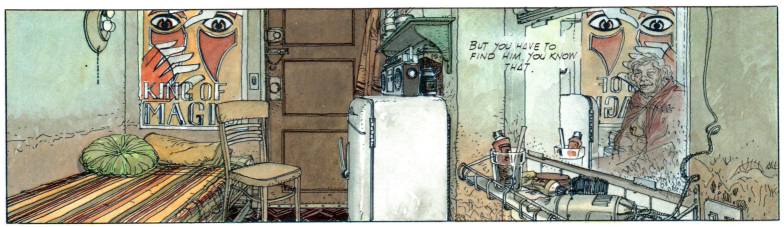

BUT YOU HAVE TO FIND HIM, YOU KNOW THAT.

HE'S HORRIBLE, BUT YOU MUST LOVE HIM. YOU'RE NOTHING WITHOUT EDMUND.

KEEP QUIET, MAMA! YOU CAN'T SAY THAT, NOT YOU!

NO!!

She wandered across deserted streets and avenues packed with people.

The odor of sweat and gasoline drove her into the dark silence of Central Park.

The simple haze of the moon softened Rita's memories.

WELL, LOOK WHO'S HERE?!

RITA!... NICE TO SEE YA, BABY. OUT FOR A NATURE WALK?

IT'S NOT TOO BRIGHT TO BE HERE WITHOUT THE HOOK! THIS PLACE HAS A BAD REPUTATION. YOU COULD STEP INTO SOME DEEP SHIT.

LET'S TAKE HER MONEY, ROSS.

LATER. I'VE GOT A BETTER IDEA... HOW'D YA LIKE A LITTLE GANG BANG IN THE WOODS?

YOU'D GO FOR THAT, WOULDN'T YOU, BITCH? YEAH, MAKING IT WITH THREE HOT STUDS... AND YOU CAN DO ME FIRST.

HEY, BOSS, SAVE ME A PIECE!

AND LOOK WHAT SHE'S HIDING UNDER THERE!

KISS ME, YOU LITTLE WHORE.

WHO'S THERE?...

EDMUND?? IS THAT YOU, EDMUND?

CHAPTER 3

I KNOW A CUNT WHO'D BETTER NOT BREATHE A WORD TO THE COPS!...

YEAH, SHE GOT LUCKY THE OTHER NIGHT. I'M A PATIENT GUY, BUT I'M TELLIN' YA, I'LL MAKE HER PISS BLOOD.

BETTER COOL IT, ROSS...

... THE GIRL IS WEIRD.

SOMETHING PULLED RITA TO CENTRAL PARK; WAS IT THE MOON, OR EDMUND'S GHOST?

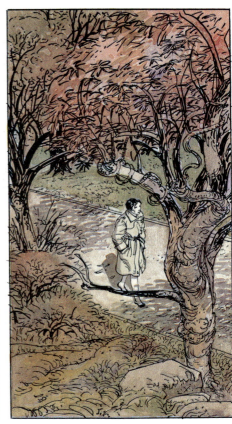

EDMUND?!! IS THAT YOU, EDMUND?

SURE, WHY NOT? HAVE A SMOKE AND LET'S TALK A BIT.

I'VE GOT MONEY TO BURN.

YOU LOOK LIKE A GORGEOUS PIECE. YOU MUST BE A PRO OR ELSE YOU DO TRICKS ONCE IN A WHILE... I DON'T CARE. WE CAN GET REAL DIRTY IF YOU WANT. I'M NOT PARTICULAR.

It's not a pretty sight.

Limbs torn apart, big hole in the chest, just like the other one. Must be the same nut who did it.

Anything on the victim at headquarters?

Name's Ferguson. A prowler. Picked up a couple of times on a morals rap.

Hey Verbone, how's my favorite french detective? What do you make of all this?

Wha...?!

THIS ISN'T PARIS, WHERE YOU CAN WALK AROUND IN A TRANCE. THE MAYOR WANTS RESULTS. WHAT'S WITH YOUR FAMOUS SIXTH SENSE? YOU'VE SOLVED HUNDREDS OF CRIMES LIKE THIS, EH, VERBONE?

INSPECTOR VERBONE, ANY NEWS FOR US? DO WE HAVE ANOTHER JACK THE RIPPER ON OUR HANDS?

I'VE GOT NOTHING TO SAY, OLD BOY. I'M JUST A GUEST.

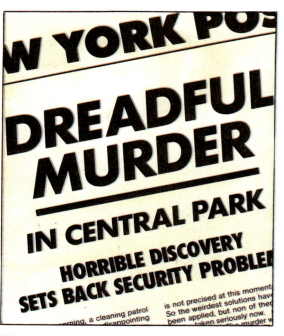

W YORK POS
DREADFUL MURDER
IN CENTRAL PARK

HORRIBLE DISCOVERY
SETS BACK SECURITY PROBLEM

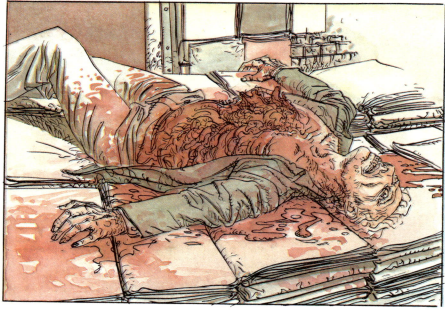

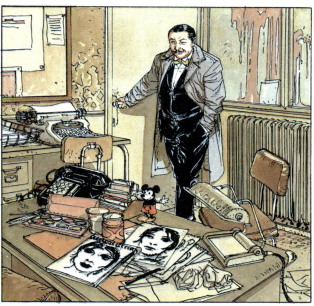

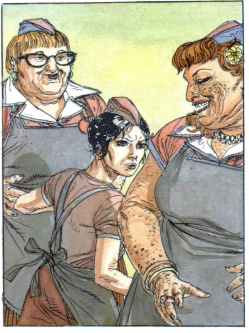

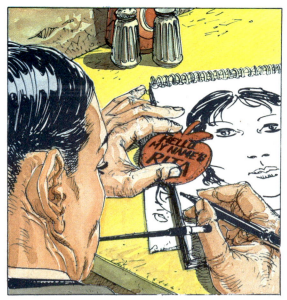

I HAD A SWEETHEART IN 'NAM. HER FAMILY WAS WIPED OUT IN A RAID... I WANTED TO BRING HER BACK WITH ME.

SHE WAS BEAUTIFUL. I LOVED HER. I PROTECTED HER FROM ALL THE FREAKS IN 'NAM... YOU REMIND ME OF HER, MISS RITA.

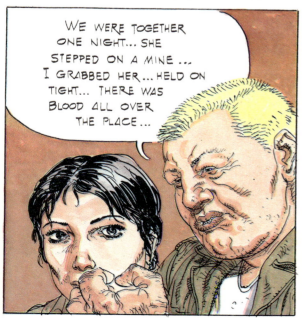

WE WERE TOGETHER ONE NIGHT... SHE STEPPED ON A MINE... I GRABBED HER... HELD ON TIGHT... THERE WAS BLOOD ALL OVER THE PLACE...

... THIS IS WHAT I GOT!

PEOPLE TELL ME THAT IF YOU LOSE A HAND, IT DOESN'T DIE RIGHT AWAY...

SOMETIMES I CAN FEEL MY HAND HOLDING HERS.

How do you like your coffee? ...Strong?

That's how I like it. Very, very strong.

...Who are you?

Who are we, you ought to say. That's a good start! I like metaphysical questions.

Let's just say I'm the man who came to make your coffee...

Or maybe I'm the new tenant of the apartment upstairs and I landed on the wrong floor...those kinds of answers don't upset the order of the world.

You know, people aren't really like the image they try to project... They ignore their own mystery, for the most part. Careful, the coffee's very hot.

People can take on the most incredible shapes... and one needs special powers to pierce their wall of illusion...

A little sugar?!...

DON'T WORRY, IT'S DEAD...

WE HAD A LITTLE ARGUMENT BEFORE YOU ARRIVED... SPITEFUL ANIMAL, BUT I WON.

YOU MUST HAVE FRIENDS WHO LIKE TO GIVE YOU UNUSUAL GIFTS... I'D SUGGEST YOU ASK AROUND FOR A RELIABLE EXTERMINATOR...

A SCORPION CAN END HIS OWN CAREER BY STINGING HIMSELF... IT'S A CHINESE PROVERB I JUST INVENTED!

YOU HAVE THINGS TO LEARN ABOUT YOURSELF. BE CAREFUL.

VERBONE !!!

I WANT TO SPEAK TO VERBONE! I'VE GOT SOME INFORMATION!

WHAT'S GOING ON? WHO'S MAKING THAT RACKET?

WE PICKED UP THREE DRIFTERS IN THE PARK LAST NIGHT. THEY MUST BE IN LOVE WITH YOU. THEY KEEP YELLING YOUR NAME...

HEY, ROSS, LOOKS LIKE YOU WERE WALKING AROUND WITH SOME OLD LADIES' PURSES. YOU'VE CHANGED SPECIALTIES, OLD BOY.

VERBONE, I KNOW A FEW THINGS...

... IF YOU LET US OUT, I'LL TELL YOU WHO'S BEEN SHREDDING THOSE PEOPLE IN THE PARK.

O.K.! I'M LISTENING...

... THE ONE YOU WANT IS A WAITRESS AT WILLY'S, WHERE ALL THE COPS GO TO EAT. SHE LOOKS LIKE A SAINT, BUT SHE'S A REGULAR WITCH!

OH, REALLY?! AND I SUPPOSE YOU HAVE SOME PROOF?...

YOU DON'T BELIEVE ME!... LOOK! SHE WAS A WEREWOLF IN A CIRCUS!... I FOUND THIS AT HER PLACE!

WEREWOLF ON STAGE!

AH... AHA!

I ALSO FOUND SOMETHING AT HER PLACE... REMIND YOU OF SOMEONE?

OH SHIT! POPEYE! HE'S WASTED MY POPEYE!

NEXT TIME TAKE BETTER CARE OF YOUR PETS. SHOULDN'T LET THEM OUT OF YOUR SIGHT, UNLESS THEY'RE ON A LONG LEASH.

HEY, FRENCHIE, YOU'RE NOT GONNA LEAVE ME HERE?!!

VERBONE, YOU PROMISED!! SON OF A BITCH! I CAN'T STAY HERE. I'LL DIE. DO YOU HEAR ME, VERBONE!

ROSS, HE DOESN'T GIVE A SHIT.

RITA! DON'T GO BACK IN THE PARK...

IT'S DANGEROUS FOR YOU. FULL OF TRAPS AND ILLUSIONS...

63

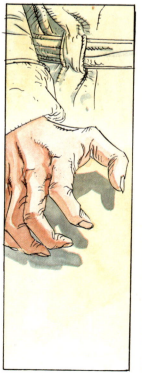

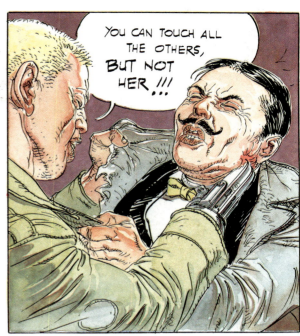

You O.K., Verbone? Great job! They'll probably make you king of Paris.

If... if you are done... speaking... if you have any saliva left, call me an ambulance.

Ri... Rita!...

I... I can't... take... care of you... anymore...

SOME WEEKS LATER

Yes? Come in!

GREETINGS! NO MORE SCORPIONS OR OTHER CREATURES TO WORRY ABOUT TODAY?

VERBONE! I WAS WONDERING IF I'D EVER SEE YOU AGAIN.

WOULD HAVE COME SOONER, BUT I'VE HAD A FEW PROBLEMS WITH MY HEALTH.

FROM THE LOOK OF THINGS, I'D SAY YOU'RE ABOUT TO GO SOMEWHERE.

CAN'T YOU EVER STOP BEING A COP?

IT'S JUST THAT... WELL, IT'S IN MY BLOOD. I NEED A BREAK, TOO, AND SARATOGA IS SUPPOSED TO BE WONDERFUL IN THE SNOW.

BUT I DIDN'T COME HERE TO PLAY GAMES. I HAVE SOMETHING FOR YOU.

HELLO MY NAME IS RITA

THANKS, BUT I DON'T REALLY NEED THIS ANY MORE.

WELL, YOU NEVER KNOW!

69

PSSST! HEY, PRINCESS! GOING TO SARATOGA, TOO?

YOU LIVE THERE?...

NO, I'M GOING TO LOOK FOR SOMEONE.

...I'M STAYING AT THE CAROLINE ON CIRCULAR STREET, IT'S A RETIREMENT HOME... FOR JOCKEYS.

THIS TIME OF THE YEAR IT'S VERY QUIET. I LIKE TO GO TO NEW YORK FOR FUN! THE CAROLINE IS LIKE A MORGUE.

... THE DIRECTOR'S A PAIN IN THE ASS. YEAH, DOLORES...USED TO BE A HOOKER. STINKS WORSE THAN DEATH. SHE LOVES TO STEAL OUR MONEY...

BUT I'M NOT SUCH AN EASY MARK. BROADWAY...THAT'S WHERE I SPEND MY DOUGH.

YORK-SARATO

RITA! WAKE UP, WE'VE ARRIVED IN SARATOGA!

NOW THAT WE'RE MARRIED, THE HOUSE ON CIRCULAR STREET BELONGS TO US.

THEN CAN I WATER THE FLOWERS IN THE GARDEN?

YOU CAN WATER WHATEVER YOU LIKE!

70

CHAPTER 4

LA FEMME DU MAGICIEN
IV

SARATOGA SPRINGS 1973

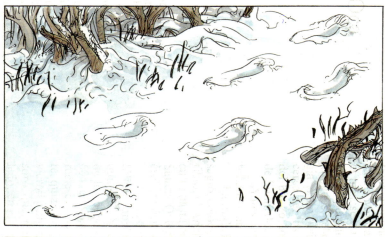

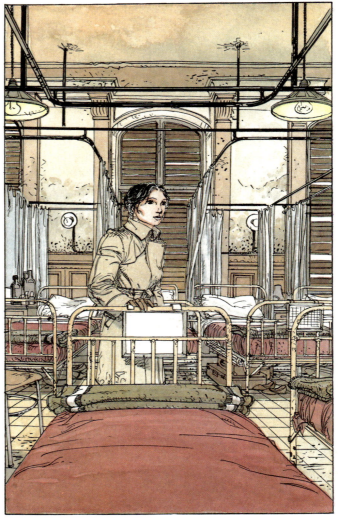

HEY !!... WHAT ARE YOU DOING HERE ?

YOU'RE ON THE WRONG FLOOR, SWEETHEART. BAD MOVE. THE LITTLE OLD MEN AROUND HERE CAN TAKE CARE OF THEM-SELVES... AND THEIR DOUGH.

I'M NOT A THIEF!

I REMEMBER NOW! YOU WERE ON THE BUS WITH ME FROM NEW YORK!

SO WHAT'S A GOOD LOOKER DOIN' IN A DUMP LIKE THIS?

I USED TO LIVE HERE!

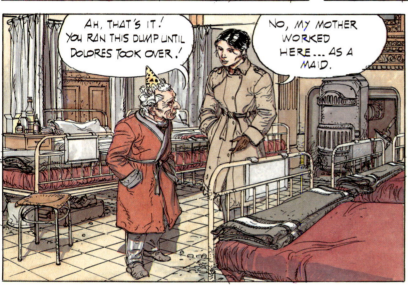

AH, THAT'S IT! YOU RAN THIS DUMP UNTIL DOLORES TOOK OVER!

NO, MY MOTHER WORKED HERE... AS A MAID.

THEN YOU'RE PRACTICALLY ONE OF US! COME ALONG AND I'LL INTRODUCE YOU TO THE BOYS...

WE'RE IN THE MIDDLE OF A BIRTHDAY PARTY...

AND DON'T TAKE THIS TOO SERIOUSLY, PRINCESS. WE'RE LIKE KIDS. AT OUR AGE, BIRTHDAYS MEAN A LOT.

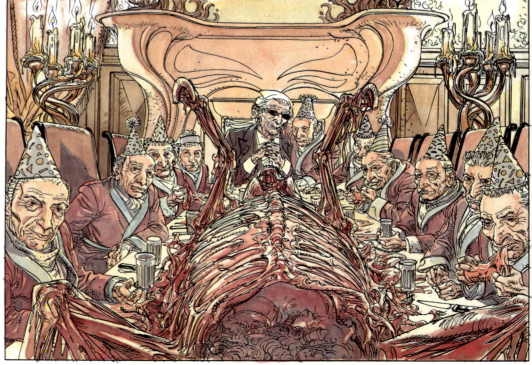

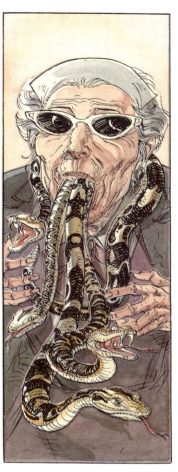

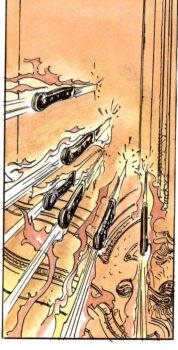

RITA, I'M FINISHED!...

I KNEW YOU'D COME BACK, RITA. I WAS WAITING FOR YOU.

WHY HAVE YOU BECOME A SLAVE TO THAT HORRIBLE WOMAN AND THOSE LITTLE MEN?

I COULDN'T HELP MYSELF. THE WOMAN IS POWERFUL.

... I'M ONLY A TRICKSTER WITHOUT YOU.

LISTEN! SOMEONE'S COMING!

IT'S NOTHING. JUST THE SNOW CREAKING AGAINST THE GLASS.

EDMUND!!!